UNfabulous

Keepin' It Real!

Keepin' It Real!

Adapted by Robin Wasserman

Based on "The Party" and "The Secret"
Teleplays by Sue Rose and Laura McCreary

Based on *Unfabulous* created by Sue Rose

SCHOLASTIC INC.

New York   Toronto   London   Auckland   Sydney
Mexico City   New Delhi   Hong Kong   Buenos Aires

ISBN 0-439-79666-0

Published by Scholastic Inc. All rights reserved.
SCHOLASTIC and associated logos are trademarks and/or registered trademarks of Scholastic Inc.

12 11 10 9 8 7 6 5 4 3 2 1   5 6 7 8 9/0
Printed in the U.S.A.
First printing, September 2005

You know how sometimes things don't turn out the way you think they're going to?

How something that sounds like a bad idea can turn out to be a good idea?

But then something happens that makes you think you were right the first time and it really *was* a bad idea?

Welcome to my life.

Don't believe me? Here's a perfect example. Picture it: an awesome party, a room filled with balloons, streamers, mood lighting, pumping music, all the junk food you could ever want to eat — and *everyone* I know. They're all having a great time, laughing, talking, dancing, stuffing their faces . . . a few of the brave girls are even talking to boys.

And then there's me, Addie Singer.

Facedown.

In a punch bowl.

Like I say, welcome to my life.

How did I end up in a punch bowl? Well, maybe I'm a little klutzy. Maybe, like my obnoxious older brother, Ben, says, a little spazz-tastic. But that was the *old* me. The unfabulous me. This year I decided that I was done with all that. Seventh grade was going to be different. *I* was going to be different. Starting from the very first day of school at Rocky Road Middle School. Day 1 of the new and Improved Addie Singer.

I walked through the front door of school with my two best friends, Geena Fabiano and Zach Carter-Schwartz, by my side. I couldn't wait to show everyone how much I'd changed in just three months.

The hallway was filled with kids, all laughing and catching up with one another. But as soon as I walked through the door, they were all in awe.

"Whoa! Who's that cool-looking girl with Geena and Zach?" said one kid.

"No. Way." Patti Perez, the most beautiful, most popular girl in school, came up behind him. She looked like her eyes were going to fall out of her head. "That's Addie Singer!"

Zach and Geena linked arms with me, glowing with pride. They wanted the whole school to know that they were my friends. I just kept my head high and pretended I couldn't hear all the people shouting things like "Wow, Addie, you look great!" and "Addie, you're so much cooler than you were last year!"

After all, I didn't want to brag. Just because I'd suddenly turned into the coolest girl in town didn't mean I was going to get a big head about it. I was still the same old Addie Singer. Just . . . better.

Besides, I had bigger things to think about than my adoring fans. Because there he was, off on the fringes of the crowd.

Jake Behari. Shaggy brown hair, deep brown eyes, perfect smile. He was a starting player on the Rocky Road Middle School soccer team, even though he was only a seventh grader . . . and Jake was the crush of my life since — well, since forever. I just knew he was perfect for me. Even though we never had an actual conversation. And this year, that was finally about to change.

"Hey, Addie! Addie!" he called, jumping up and down and waving to me.

"Jake!" I called, pushing my way through the crowd. But the crowd was pushing back, carrying me away down the hall. Away from Jake.

"Addie!" he cried, his voice getting more and more distant.

"Jake!" I yelled as Geena and Zach swept me down the hall. I felt like everything was moving in slow motion, like I was watching them carry me away and I knew I was powerless to stop it. "You guys, turn around," I urged them. "It's Jake! Jake!"

But they wouldn't listen. Jake tried his best to follow, crying out for me to stop.

"Addie!"

"Jake!"

"Addie!"

"Can't we stop and talk to him?" I begged Geena.

She turned to me with a sad face, shook her head, and opened her mouth to respond.

"Addie, WOOF."

Uh, excuse me?

"WOOF WOOF WOOF WOOF — WOOF!"

And then I woke up.

Nancy, my slightly overweight, golden-haired, fluffy mutt of a dog, was standing on my chest and barking in my face.

"Nancy!" I complained, wiping her drool off my chin and squirming away from her stinky dog breath, "Why can't you ever wait until *after* Jake Behari declares me his soul mate? Don't you want me to be happy?"

Nancy just wagged her tail and gave me one of

those "Aren't I lovable?" looks that I can never resist. I ruffled the soft fur along her belly (she loves that) and then pushed her off the bed. Officially, she's not allowed on top of the covers — Mom's afraid she'll mess up my comforter. Unofficially? It's her favorite place in the house.

Who knows? I figured as I flipped through my closet, searching desperately for something perfect to wear. Maybe just this once, my dreams would come true.

See, that's the thing about me — I like to look on the bright side. I always figure things are about to take a turn for the better.

Which brings me to one more thing you should know about me: I'm almost always wrong.

"Gold eye shadow on the first day of school?" I took the little pink cell phone I was talking on away from my ear and gave it a look. It was the look I always give Geena (even when she isn't around) when she forgets that she's just a student at Rocky Road Middle School — and not the star of her own music video.

She forgets a lot.

"Too much too soon," I warned her, putting the phone back to my ear. "We have two hundred and eighty-three days of seventh grade. Pace yourself."

Geena was starting to say something about first impressions and how it was our year to make a big splash . . . but I wasn't listening. It's hard to pay attention when your big brother is rushing down the hallway, knocking you out of the way, throwing himself into the bathroom, and flashing you the "loser" sign on his fore-head before slamming the door in your face.

"Geena, gotta go," I said quickly. "See you in a few." I snapped the phone shut and started banging on the door, furious.

"Ben, you don't even need to be in there!" I shouted. "Your school doesn't start until next week!"

It's so unfair. You'd think that sharing a bathroom with your brother wouldn't be a big deal. After all, most high school boys, *normal* high school boys, couldn't care less about how they look. But my big brother? Well, how can I put this? He's just not normal.

Ben thinks he's the center of the universe — and it doesn't help that all the girls in his school agree with him. Ben is like the total opposite of me. He's always been pop-ular, without even trying. Even *my* friends think he's cool (although they promise he's not cooler than me). Geena's always saying that he's totally hot, which I think is gross. After all, to me, he's just Ben. Annoying, obsessed with himself — and now he'd picked the worst possible moment to lock himself in the bathroom. It was the first day of seventh grade, and I needed all the time I could get to make myself look fabulous. Was he *trying* to ruin my life?

"Let me in!" I shouted again, whacking my fists against the door.

"Can't let you in without the password," he said from the other side of the door. I could just imagine the stupid grin on his face.

Okay, enough was enough. Suddenly, I caught a glimpse of the phone sitting on our hall table, right outside the bathroom, and I got a brilliantly devious idea. I whipped out my cell phone again and dialed a familiar number. Ever since Ben's girlfriend, Tara, moved to California, he's been a lot easier to handle — and to fool. I guess love will do that to you.

I pressed TALK, and our home phone started ringing. Grabbing the receiver, I pretended there was someone on the other end.

"Hello? Oh, hi, *Tara*," I said loudly. "No, Ben can't talk, he's in the bathroom counting his chest hairs. Three more than last week!"

Right on cue, the bathroom door flew open. Ben dove for the phone, but I dangled it out of reach.

"Gimme that, you little —" He ripped the phone out of my hand and then, taking a deep breath, spoke into the mouthpiece in his best "smooth operator" voice. It's about two octaves lower than his real one. "Hey, babe! Miss me already?" There was a pause, and he looked confused. "Hello?"

Much as I would have loved to watch the show — nothing's funnier than the look on Ben's face when he realizes he's been had — there was no time for gloating. Slipping past him, I dove into the bathroom, slamming the door behind me. I locked it and heaved a sigh of relief, then grinned and lifted my cell phone to my ear.

"Thanks for the bathroom!" I chirped, and then hung up.

"Hope you like it in there!" he shouted, pounding the door. "'Cause you better not come out!" He banged on the door once more for good measure, then finally I heard him stomping off down the hall.

Winning feels *so* good.

Usually I'm not much of a morning person. Okay, that's the understatement of the year. Usually, I'm half asleep until noon — and that's on a good day. But that morning, I was wide awake and bursting with energy. Why? Because this wasn't just any first day of school — it was the first day of *seventh grade.* It was like a whole new world. I mean, everything looked the same — same school, same hair, same clothes — but still, I felt ... different. New and Improved, remember?

Besides, seventh grade was going to be *so* much better than sixth. We already knew the important stuff, like where the bathrooms were and which teachers smelled like vitamins. Also, this year we were allowed to take a creative elective. I'd been waiting for years to finally be able to take music composition. I taught myself how to play the guitar when I was nine, and I've probably written a song about every important occasion of my life ever since.

Like when I turned thirteen and my parents threw me a big party:

> *I can't drive, and I can't vote,*
> *I can't even pierce my nose,*
> *So what does it mean ... to be thirteen?*
> *I can go to the movies and see ... PG Thirteen!*
> *(Can't see it when you're twelve!)*
> *PG Thirteen!*
> *PG Thirteen!*
> *PG Thirteen!*

Or the time that I ate a tuna fish sandwich that had been sitting out on the counter just a little too long:

Tossed my cookies on a yellow bus,
Bus Driver Bob, he sure did cuss.
At least I got to stay home,
That's the upside of food poisoning.

And if you liked those, you'll love this one. It's called "New Shoes":

New shoes, you rule!
You rule, new shoes!
New shoes, you rule!
You rule, new shoes!

So maybe I'm not going to win a Grammy any time soon. But you know what? I don't care. When I'm sitting in my bedroom with my guitar, I don't have to worry what anyone thinks of me. Nobody's watching me, nobody's judging me. I can just sing whatever pops into my head — I can say *anything*. It's the only time I can be completely myself.

Geena and Zach met me at my house so that we could walk to school together. They were just as excited about seventh grade as I was.

"So, how do I look?" Geena asked as soon as I

stepped outside the house. She twirled around for me, and I choked back a gasp. Geena was wearing a lime-green shirt that looked like someone had ripped off the collar and one of the sleeves. She had on about seven necklaces, and her brown curly hair fell over her face in a high side ponytail. But the real shocker, and not in a good way, was a stonewashed denim miniskirt that was about the size of a bandanna.

"How do you look? Like you left the house before your mom got to see what you were wearing," I told her, imagining the look on my mother's face if I came down-stairs in a skirt like that.

Geena beamed. "Perfect!"

Thankfully, Zach at least looked normal. Worn jeans, short-sleeve button-down shirt hanging open over a T-shirt — your standard half-laid-back, half-preppy first-day-of-seventh-grade outfit ... at least, that's what I thought at first. Then I noticed his feet. No, I don't mean his shoes — I mean his *feet*.

"Um, Zach?" I asked, wrinkling my nose. "Why are you not wearing shoes?"

Zach lifted one bare foot in midair and wiggled his toes for us to see. "Dude, shoes aren't natural," he explained. "They were just created by shoe companies for profit." He swung a fist in the air and got that dreamy-eyed look he gets when he's about to start yet another save-the-world campaign. "My ten little piggies are free range!"

"It'd be better to write thoughts like this down in a little notepad," Geena suggested. "That way you don't say them out loud and risk ruining our social life."

Um, maybe now would be a good time for me to mention that my two best friends are a little . . . weird. Well, I guess you could call them that — I prefer "lovably eccentric." It's true that they do strange things some-times — but that just makes them interesting. Besides, it's not like I'm so cookie-cutter normal myself. How bor-ing would that be?

Still, there's a time to be your weird self and ignore what everyone else thinks of you — and then there's a time to blend in and pretend that you're just an average member of the human race. The beginning of seventh grade, when I was trying to create a fabulous new image for myself, seemed one of those times.

"Zach, I don't care if I have to make you a giant pair of baby booties, you're wearing shoes when we all go to Randy Klein's party," I warned him.

But I guess my famous Addie Singer glare needs a

little work, because Zach didn't look scared. Just intrigued.

"Baby booties, that would be funny," he laughed. Then he cocked his head in confusion. "Hey, you just said 'Randy Klein' without throwing up!"

Geena rolled her eyes. "Right, Addie," she said skeptically. "Like *you're* gonna go to Randy Klein's party."

And why wouldn't I go to Randy Klein's annual back-to-school party?

Oh, I don't know, how about because I go every year — and every year, something embarrassing happens to me. Something so embarrassing that I end up with a horrible new nickname. One that sticks with me all year long.

"Hey, remember Mudzilla?" Zach asks enthusiastically.

"Mudzilla" — that's thanks to my belly flop into a big pile of mud. And, of course, "Sprinkler Bell" — that was the year I tripped and landed on top of a lawn sprinkler, setting it off. And who could forget the year Randy's parents hired a juggler — guess who got hit in the head with a flying club? That would be me: good ol' Juggy McJughead.

Back to the present day. Geena and Zach were

both still staring at me as if I'd suddenly sprouted a second head.

"You said you'd rather give pedicures to old people than go to another party at Randy Klein's," Geena reminded me.

True, but . . .

"That was before," I pointed out, standing up straight and jutting out my chin. "I was young. Foolish. Nothing bad's gonna happen this year — I'm different."

Zach gave me a slow, sly grin. "Does that mean we can call you . . ."

"Hey, *Sprinkler Bell*! Have a good summer?"

I whirled around — it was Eli Pataki, my own personal enemy. Eli is a shrimpy loudmouth who makes up in volume what he lacks in height. He sauntered up to me and, before I could escape, patted me on the head. He had to stand on his tiptoes.

Eli thinks he's funny — and I have to admit, sometimes he is. But mostly he just drives me crazy. That's why, in a perfect world, here's what would have happened next:

"How original," I observed with a sneer. Then, suddenly, I whipped around and flung out my leg in a black-belt karate kick, connecting solidly with Eli's jaw.

Thwap!

He went down like a sack of potatoes and rolled around on the ground, moaning and clutching his face.

"Sorry to spoil your fun, Eli," I said snidely. Hands on my hips, I towered over his squirming figure. "But New and Improved Addie doesn't let stupid, childish, idiotic, and stupid nicknames bother her."

Too bad it's not a perfect world. Because in this one, I don't know karate — and every time someone calls me a stupid name, my face turns bright red and I lose the ability to speak. In this world, Eli just stood there smirking at me, waiting for me to say something. Finally, I found the right words.

"Yeah, Eli, I did have a good summer." My face was painted with the fakest smile in the known universe. "Thanks for asking."

When we finally got to school, everything looked exactly as it had in my dream, right down to the welcome back banner reading WELCOME BACK, ROCKY ROAD MIDDLE SCHOOL STUDINTS! (And just like in my dream, somebody had scrawled "And Teachers!" underneath.) As we pushed our way through the front doors, I spotted Mario by his locker. Suddenly, his eyes widened and he pointed at me.

"Check it!"

Everyone turned to follow his gaze, and I caught

my breath. Could this be it? The moment that the population of Rocky Road Middle School suddenly realized that they had a secretly fabulous seventh grader in their midst? Was the New and Improved Addie really such an amazing sight?

"They spelled 'students' wrong on the banner!" Mario continued.

We all looked up at the banner — and there it was, STUDINTS, in big block letters. Geena and Zach laughed and joked about how dumb the teachers were that they couldn't even spell, and I laughed along with them. No one had to know that I was laughing at myself for actually imagining that my dream was coming true. Not that I'd given up on my New and Improved image — it was just going to take a little more time.

We headed to our lockers, where the dreaded Maris Bingham and Cranberry St. Clare were holding a popular-people powwow. Remember how I said it would be boring if all my friends were totally normal? Well, meet Maris and Cranberry. It doesn't get more "normal" than them — everything they say, do, or wear is carefully calculated to be picture-perfect average teenage behavior. They're like cardboard cutouts. They may be two of the most popular girls in school, but as far as I'm concerned, they're just boring. I mean, *listen* to them.

"And I was all 'Yes, I am.' And he was all 'No, you're not,'" Cranberry was confiding to Maris. "And I was all 'Yes. I. Am.' And he was all —"

"Cranberry, I get it," Maris cut in. (See? Even *she* was getting bored.) That's when she noticed us. "Hi, Muddie," she said in a perky voice. Muddie — that's me, of course — short for Mudzilla. Courtesy of my Randy Klein mud bath. "I mean *Addie*. Can't wait for another of your *fabulous* performances at Randy Klein's party!" she gushed. "Nick Russo is giving five-to-one odds that you'll land in something wet."

"Burn!" they shouted in unison.

Suddenly, a deluge of water dropped from the sky, soaking them. They both screamed, dripping wet from their ruined hairdos right down to their soggy shoes.

"Aaaaaah!" Maris cried, water streaming down her face.

"My hair!" Cranberry squealed, holding up the lank, sopping strands.

"I'll show you 'fabulous,' Maris and Cranberry," I informed them. "The days of making a fool of myself are history!"

Okay, so I have a rich fantasy life. But you need it

when you're dealing with clowns like this on a daily basis. And now, back to reality. Maris and Cranberry were completely dry. And still laughing. As usual, I couldn't come up with anything to say — not in the real world, at least — so I just gave them a snotty wave and walked off.

Lucky for me, Geena is a little better at the quick-thinking thing, and a *lot* better at saying what she thinks. As we walked away, she turned back to Maris and Cranberry, crinkling her nose and waving a hand in front of her face, like she smelled something rotting.

"And what are the odds you'll pop a breath mint?" she called back to them. "Just because we have to hear your stupid jokes doesn't mean we have to smell 'em, too!"

"Now *that*," Zach added while Maris and Cranberry did breath checks, "that was a *third-degree* burn!"

I was about to congratulate Geena, but she was already on to her next big issue of the day: her wardrobe.

"I don't get it," she complained. "We've been here for twenty minutes and *no one* has noticed my skirt!"

"Someone has noticed," Zach pointed out, his head swiveling toward the angry woman zooming down the hall toward us on her motorized scooter. She was in her late sixties, with a sour smile and more wrinkles than my fancy dry-clean-only party dress got the day I accidentally washed it. If you didn't know any better, you might look at her flowery dress and her graying hair and think she was someone's grandmother, about to offer you a fresh-baked chocolate chip cookie. But, unfortunately for us, *we* knew better.

That was no one's grandmother. That was our principal, Agatha Brandywine. You know that saying "The principal is your *pal*"? Well, maybe that's *your* principal. Principal Brandywine wasn't happy unless she was giving someone a detention — and Geena made her *very* happy.

"Ms. Fabiano, must I remind you this is a hall of learning and *not* the Hoochie Room at the Rock and Roll Motel!" she carped, shaking a ruler at Geena. I'd seen that ruler plenty of times before — in her free time, Principal Brandywine liked to stalk the halls in search of short skirts. Her special ruler measured the distance between your knee and your hemline. It had three markings: ACCEPTABLE, WARNING, . . . and GEENA.

Guess how Geena's skirt measured up.

Principal Brandywine triumphantly whipped out her pad of pink detention slips and handed one to Geena.

"Ah, nothing says 'back to school' like a crisp new pad of pink slips," she sighed, giving us her first real smile of the year. With a loud whirring noise, her scooter puttered off down the hall — right over Zach's bare foot.

"Aaah!" he yelped, grabbing his foot and hopping around like a spastic frog.

Geena and I just pretended we didn't know him. That's what you get for coming to school barefoot, right?

We only had a few more minutes until our first class of the day, and I dashed over to the water fountain to grab a drink before it was time to go. But as I pressed the button that sent a spout of water spurting toward my face, something caught my eye. And instead of drinking, I just stared.

There he was — the real reason I wanted to go to Randy Klein's party. Jake Behari.

I'd known Jake for years and never said a single word to him. But this year, that was all going to change. This year, I resolved, I was going to talk to Jake Behari someplace other than in my dreams.

"Hey, Juggy McJughead," the kid behind me complained, poking me lightly in the back. "Sometime today?"

I turned around to see a long line of kids waiting for the water fountain to be free, and I took a quick drink before jumping out of the way. I wasn't thirsty anymore, anyway. I was still thinking about Jake, and about how this could be our year. This year, he was going to know my name.

"See ya later, Juggy!"

And I mean my *real* name.

We trooped into homeroom and took our seats — all except for Geena. Standing at her desk, she had an important question for the class: "Have you guys seen any new kids? You know, the kind that starts with 'B' and ends with 'oys'?"

I was just surprised that it had taken Geena this long — thirty-two minutes into the day, by my watch — to get down to her favorite subject. But before I could answer, the PA system dinged. We all stopped talking, fast. I know that in some schools, the morning announcements are a guaranteed snooze-fest. But in our school, Eli Pataki is behind the mike. Say what you want about Eli (and I could say a lot), but he makes mornings interesting.

"Good morning, Rocky Road Middle School!" Eli's voice boomed out, low and fast like a radio disc jockey. "Known for such classics as 'No Running in the Halls!' and

'Spit It Out in My Hand This Instant!,' heeeeeeeeeere's Priiiiiiiincipal Braaaaaaaaaaandywine!"

"I am the principal," she complained huffily, "not the opening act at the Ha Ha Café!"

What in the world was the Ha Ha Café? I bet it would have been more fun than homeroom.

"Let's see," the principal continued, clearing her throat. "Regarding this year's seventh-grade privileges. Eating lunch outside . . ."

The whole class exchanged enthusiastic glances.

"We've been waiting our whole middle school lives to eat lunch outside!" Zach exclaimed in an excited whisper, giving Mario a high five.

". . . is no longer permissible," Principal Brandywine snapped, "due to the behavior of last year's seventh graders. Anyone knowing the whereabouts of our mascot statue, please contact my office. No questions asked."

No outside lunch? What was the point of being a seventh grader if you couldn't eat lunch outside?

"Well, at least we can hang out in the computer lab without a supervisor," I told Geena. Like I said, my policy is to look on the bright side.

"No one is allowed in the computer lab without a supervisor," Principal Brandywine's voice boomed. "Last year's class spent their time chatting."

"What about Spring Fling?" Geena asked, sounding frightened. "Ski Week?"

"There will be no Spring Fling or Ski Week," Principal Brandywine finished, as if she'd heard Geena's plea. "Remember to thank the eighth-grade hooligans when you pass them in the hall. And have a lovely year!"

Geena, Zach, and I stared at one another in horror. Seventh grade wasn't turning out quite how we'd expected it. On the other hand . . .

"At least I've still got my creative elective," I pointed out, trying to stay optimistic. Okay, so not everything was going my way, but I figured that music comp would still be awesome. There was no *way* Principal Brandywine could mess that one up for me.

Well, guess what, Addie?

Wrong again.

What did I learn on my first day of seventh grade? Here's something: Banging your head against your desk when you're frustrated doesn't make you feel any better. It just gives you a headache.

And why was I so frustrated? Apparently, music comp was now an eighth-grade-only elective. All the seventh graders who signed up for it got stuck in other

25

courses. And, since most of the good courses were already filled up, I got stuck with . . .

"The. Theory. Of. Chess," as our teacher put it as he introduced us to the class. I'd never seen him around before, but he looked exactly like you'd expect: dorky white shirt, dorky sweater vest, dorky thick-rimmed glasses. Since I'd already forgotten his name, I guess I could just think of him as Mr. Chess Dork. Big surprise: He also sounded like a robot.

"Meet the rook," he said, in a voice guaranteed to lull us all to sleep in under five minutes. He held up a random chess piece. "For the next few weeks, you will eat, breathe, and sleep — the rook."

I sighed and lay my head back down on the desk (more gently, this time). It was going to be a long year. Or so I thought — until I discovered that every dark cloud has a silver lining.

"Excuse me? Is this the chess class?"

Even in the depths of my misery, I could recognize the voice. I would have recognized it anywhere. First I thought that robo chess master had put me to sleep and I was dreaming again. But when I looked up, he was really there: Jake Behari.

Without stopping to think about what I was doing, I swept my arm across the desk of the chess geek next to me and knocked all his chess pieces to the floor. It worked like a charm. My geeky neighbor looked like he was going to cry.

"My pieces!" he exclaimed.

Since he wasn't moving fast enough, I had to knock him to the floor, too. He landed with a thud and began scrambling around, gathering up all his chess pieces. Too bad for him — excellent for me.

"Over here, Jake!" I called out with a bright smile, waving him over. "This seat's open!"

I wish.

Instead I wimped out and just gave him a big grin. Maybe if I was lucky, Jake would at least notice that I was the only other person in the class not dressed like a member of the varsity chess squad.

It was going to be a long year, all right — which meant I had plenty of time to muster my courage. Maybe someday I would get up enough nerve to actually speak to him. Hey, stranger things have happened!

I didn't know it at the time, but at the exact moment I was watching Jake enter the classroom, my brother was watching something else — himself. On his new Webcam.

"This Webcam stinks," my brother complained

into the phone, trying to get himself into position so that the tiny camera could capture his muscles in all their glory. "I'm way too small — you can't even see my triceps. I'm gonna move the computer closer to the weight bench."

Ben grabbed his computer monitor and the Webcam off the desk and began backing toward the weight bench — which worked okay, for about ten seconds. Then he took another step, and the image on the screen went dark. My brainiac brother had pulled the computer's power cord right out of the wall.

"It's not gonna reach!" Ben said, exasperated. "Nancy, go get an extension cord, the three-prong kind."

That's my brother — the laziest man alive. I mean, just because Nancy's a dog doesn't mean he has to treat her like one.

A second later, Nancy padded back into the room with exactly what Ben needed. Almost.

"Nancy, this is a two-prong!" he chided her, pulling the cord out of her mouth. "She never listens," he complained into the phone.

But seriously, would *you*?

*   *   *

Okay, back to the important stuff. Seventh grade, day one. Also known as the first day of the Year of Jake.

After a long day of classes, Geena, Zach, and I met at our lockers to dish about the day. It wasn't a pretty sight.

"It breaks my heart to say this, but seventh grade is no better than sixth," Zach moaned.

"Yeah, yeah, that's nice," I replied, too distracted to pay attention. "Jake Behari and I have a class together!" I waited for the gasps, the cheers, but Geena and Zach just stared at me. Maybe they didn't get how huge this was. "Now, when I see him at Randy Klein's party, I'll have an automatic in! An icebreaker! An —"

"You guys, we just heard the worst news ever!"

I turned around to see who could have possibly interrupted my extremely important Jake Behari story. It was Maris and Cranberry, and their legion of fans. Of course. The last thing I wanted to do was listen to anything they had to say, but . . . well, if you're going to survive in middle school, you've got to stay in the loop. So we stuck around and listened — and it's a good thing we did.

"Randy Klein had a water-skiing accident!" Maris intoned dramatically.

"Guess that means he's not having the party," Cranberry added, with a dismissive sigh.

"What!" I cried. "You guys are overreacting. He probably just twisted an ankle."

Okay, maybe I sounded a little heartless. I mean, of course I feel bad for Randy and all. But this was my *social life* we were talking about here. This was my chance to show off the New and Improved Addie to the world. And did I mention, my chance to hang with *Jake Behari*?

Randy couldn't let a little thing like a sprained ankle or a broken wrist or whatever it was stop him from throwing the party of the year. Could he?

No way. So Geena, Zach, and I trooped down to the hospital to tell him so.

"Hey, Randy," I said once we'd found his room, giving him a little wave. "We brought you a plant." Geena held up the potted pachysandra we'd sneaked out of her mother's garden. "You're not gonna let a little thing like this keep you from having your party . . . right?"

Randy didn't say anything. Maybe it was because he was thinking things over. Or maybe it was because, covered by a head-to-toe body cast, with all his arms and legs strung up in traction, it was a little tough for him to talk.

I leaned down close, so I was staring right in his

eyes (which happened to be the only part of his body not covered in plaster). He looked like a mummy.

"So, about the party?" I repeated hopefully. "Blink once for yes and twice for no."

That was it. All hope was gone. And so was my best shot with Jake. When I got home, I was so depressed that I ran straight up to my room and slammed the door. Then I grabbed my guitar and plopped down on my bed. When life is this bad, there's only one thing that makes me feel better.

The party's over,

I sang.

The dream is shattered.
I'm so depressed.
No one will ever know that I'm New and Improved.
I wish the party could move. . . .

That's when Nancy, who was lying at my feet, interrupted me with a long and loud howl. "Aaaaaaaaaa-wwwwwwwwooooooooooo!"

First I thought she was commenting on my

singing — but it's not *that* bad. And then I realized she was trying to tell me something. Something brilliant!

"You're right, Nancy," I cried, giving her a big bear hug. (Or, I guess in her case, a dog hug.) "Why not? Why can't I just have the party here?"

And just like that, I was singing a different tune. Literally.

I've really changed, got a new attitude,
and everyone will see it, too.
I'll take control, have no fear,
'Cause I'm gonna have the party here!

First thing the next morning, I told Zach and Geena about Nancy's amazing idea. It seemed so obvious to me now — and so perfect.

"If I have the party at my house, *I* control the environment!" I exclaimed as we walked down the hall. This just kept getting better and better. "That way, I eliminate any chance for mishaps, like too-tall sprinklers or flying bowling pins. That's a great idea, right?"

Zach was beaming. "Awesome idea," he agreed. "I call DJ."

"And I call the chocolate-covered unicorn flying on rainbow wings," Geena added sarcastically, rolling her eyes and stopping us in our tracks. "Hello? Earth to Addie and Zach. You can't just decide to have the seventh-grade kickoff party at your house. You have to go before the Party Review Board."

Zach and I gaped at each other.

"Party Review Board?" we echoed in unison.

It was the first I'd ever heard of such a thing. (See what I mean about staying in the loop? It's *essential.*) Good thing I've got Geena around for these things. So no problem, I figured. I'd just go before the Party Review Board, whatever that was, and explain to them that my basement would make a picture-perfect spot for a party. How hard could that be?

I was about to find out.

The Party Review Board held court after school in room 101. And apparently, I wasn't the only seventh grader who wanted to appear before it and plead my case. By the time Addie, Zach, and I showed up, there was already a line of kids waiting to get inside the room. Some of them had posters, others had platters of sample food — I think I even saw one girl with a huge 3-D diorama. All we had was a short stack of CDs and a piece of poster board with some hand-drawn stars and pictures of my family's basement. No way could we compete.

Just as my heart was sinking, the door opened. Some seventh grader I didn't know wheeled a cart of food out into the hall, with Maris and Cranberry following close behind. Before sending him on his way, they gave him a big hug.

"Fabulous chocolate soufflé, Kevin!" Maris gushed. "We'll call you." She said that last part under her breath, but I heard every word. And if I hadn't, Cranberry would have tipped me off when she thanked him for his present of gift certificates and "sparkly things." Maris and Cranberry were a little like babies — or birds. They loved anything that sparkled.

I was *so* out of my league.

I started to back away, pulling Geena and Zach down the hall with me. No way was I going in there and making a fool of myself in front of Maris and Cranberry.

"I can't make chocolate soufflé," I said in a panicky voice. "I don't even know what soufflé is!"

Geena dragged me back into line.

"Forget about that," she insisted. "All you need for a fun party is loud music and junk food. Your basement is perfect!"

I wanted to believe her, I really did. Especially after all the work we'd put into our presentation. Maybe, just maybe, the Party Review Board would look beyond all the messy details and realize that I was the best person in the whole school to throw this party. (Other than

Randy Klein, of course, but people in body casts didn't count.) Maybe they'd take one look at me and give me the official go-ahead.

Right — and maybe Principal Brandywine would come to school the next day dressed as a circus clown.

We waited around for hours, but we finally got in to see the board. They had pulled some desks together into a long conference table at the front of the room. Zach, Geena, and I sat on one side, and on the other? Maris, Cranberry, and — I gasped in surprise. And horror. The leader of the Party Review Board was none other than Patti Perez.

"Oh, no," I whispered to Geena, "we're sunk."

Now, let me explain something to you. Maris and Cranberry may be popular, but compared to Patti Perez? They're nothing. It's like she's their queen or something — they follow her around wherever she goes, dress like her, act like her.

This was going to be even tougher than I'd expected.

Geena, Zach, and I laid out our case, complete with diagrams and photos of my *basement*. Maris and Cranberry looked like I was a pile of mud they wanted to wipe away. Patti, who was filing her nails, just looked bored.

"Are you actually proposing we have our seventh-grade kickoff party in a basement?" Maris asked. She said the word *basement* as if it tasted like liverwurst.

"Well, it's actually our family room," I babbled, thinking fast. "My grandma used to host bingo there." Uh-oh — not fast enough to stop myself from saying the words *grandma* and *bingo* when I was trying to sound cool.

"Is this . . ." Cranberry used a pencil to point at one of the photos, so she wouldn't have to touch it herself. "Shag carpeting?" She wrinkled her nose, repulsed.

"I guess so," I said, hanging my head. This was a stupid, stupid idea.

Maris pushed her chair back from the table and gave us a little wave out of the room. "Yeah, thanks for coming, but —"

"She can have the party at her house."

It took us all a moment to realize that *Patti* had said it — after all, she hadn't even looked up from filing her nails.

Maris and Cranberry whipped their heads around to look at their fearless leader, their eyes wide and mouths agape. She'd said it, all right, and what Patti says, goes. I tried to stop myself from laughing — I was afraid that anything I said or did might make her change her mind.

Patti finally looked up from polishing off her manicure and shrugged her shoulders.

"Hello?" she said to the girls, shaking her head as if she couldn't believe how dense they were. "She has a hottie brother."

Maris and Cranberry grinned in sudden understanding, and I said a silent thank-you to my parents for having Ben. For the first time in a *long* time, I was glad I wasn't an only child. (Just don't tell Ben!)

I couldn't stop glowing. And from the look on Geena's and Zach's faces, they were feeling pretty much the same way.

"I can't believe I'm having the party at my house!" I cried, once we'd made it safely down the hall.

"I can't believe your parents are *letting* you have the party at your house," Zach added.

Oh.

Right.

Oops.

"My parents, well, um . . ." I looked away, but there was no escaping their stares.

"Addie," Geena began sternly, "did you not ask your parents yet?"

Zach shook his head ruefully. "Parents hate when you wait until the last minute to ask for something," he reminded me. "Mine need a week's notice and I gotta submit it in writing. I hope you have a plan."

Uh . . . a plan? Well, I had a Plan B:

I opened the door to find yet another guest eager to come inside and experience my fabulous once-in-a-lifetime party. It was, in fact, the best back-to-school party ever.

"Your parents must be pretty cool to let you have this party," the kid commented, looking around at the entranceway, strung up with lights and filled with party-crazed teens.

"Totally." I grinned, thinking what a brilliant daughter I was to have figured it all out. "Let me take your jacket."

He gave me his jacket and I opened the door of the closet — only to find my mom and dad sitting on the floor, back to back, tied together with a thick length of rope. Oh, that's right, I'd almost forgotten that this was the closet I was keeping them in. Oh, well — I tossed the jacket inside, and it landed on top of Dad's head. He looked like he wanted to say something but I quickly shut the door.

Um, okay, maybe not.

Plan B was out, which meant I needed to come up with a Plan A. Stat.

"I was scared, okay?" I tried to defend myself to my friends. "I was afraid they'd say no!"

But now I was more than afraid. I was terrified.

Geena patted me on the shoulder and did what all good best friends do in these kinds of situations: told me to chill out.

"Come on, parents are totally easy," she assured me. "All you gotta do is tell them what they want to hear."

Tell them what they want to hear? I considered it for a moment, then nodded firmly. I could totally do that. Piece of cake.

"So since Randy Klein can't have the party at his house, I was thinking maybe we could have it here." I looked up at my mother's face and held my breath, waiting for her to deliver the verdict.

"A party sounds like fun," my mother said with a smile.

Victory! That was way easier than I'd thought it would be. Of course, I wasn't done yet — there were just a few details that needed to be ironed out. *Just remember,* I warned myself, *tell them what they want to hear.*

"You'll have to stay upstairs," I explained. "And no flushing the toilet, you can hear it in the basement."

My dad, who was replacing a lightbulb and pretending not to listen, winced. And I could tell from the look on his face that it was definitely *not* what he'd wanted to hear. But, even though her smile got a little smaller, my mother nodded.

"Uh-huh," she agreed. "We'll be here if you need us."

Okay, I told myself. *We're almost there — now just tell them something good that will make them feel better. Tell them there will be clowns, maybe jugglers.*

"There's gonna be girls . . . and boys," I warned.

What? My dad's face went white — like, literally, white as a blizzard. Why were these words coming out of my mouth? Okay, okay, it was too much.

Ignore that, I instructed myself. *Focus on the good part. Focus on the party.*

"You know, Addie, you're thirteen years old," my mom continued. "We trust you. Just let us know if there's anything we can do."

"But, Mom —" I protested. Then I realized what she'd said. She trusts me! She believes in me! She wants me to have the back-to-school party of my dreams!

There was only one thing to do now: Run away before they changed their minds.

"Uh, thanks, great," I said quickly. "Gotta go!"

I ran upstairs as fast as I could — but not so fast that I didn't hear the loud *THUD* right after I turned my back. I didn't have to look to know what it was. My dad, collapsing to the floor at the thought of his little girl having a grown-up party.

That made me think about coming to a party at *my* house.

And that made *me* want to collapse.

But there was no time for that — I had a party to plan.

New and Improved Superfabulous life? I thought. *Ready or not, here I come!*

"This is a disaster!" I stood in the middle of my basement, ready to party. I was wearing my favorite T-shirt — tight and gray, with SOCIAL written across the front in big pink letters and my polka-dot pink skirt. Throw in a chunky bracelet and my funky star-shaped earrings, and I was ready to go. Geena, in a shiny gold shirt and black capris, was arranging trays of snacks, and Zach was digging through his CD collection searching for the perfect combination of songs. Everything was perfect. There was just one problem.

No one was there.

The room was totally, completely, one hundred percent empty. It was the humiliation of a lifetime. I'd never live it down.

"I should've known no one wanted to hang out in a basement! What kind of friends are you guys?" I asked accusingly. "Why didn't you stop me?" Shoulders slumped, I gestured listlessly at the heaping tables of food. "Just wrap up some taquitos and bagelettes and go home," I told them.

Geena put a comforting hand on my shoulder and offered up her tray of snacks. "Addie, chill."

Easy for her to say — it wasn't her reputation going down the tubes.

"It's only five," she pointed out. "The party doesn't start until six-thirty."

Oh — that's right.

Okay, so I was a little jumpy. Can you blame me? It was my first party as a seventh grader, and I wanted everything to go exactly right. And, given my experience with back-to-school parties, you can see why I might have been just a little worried. But not this time around, I reminded myself. This time was going to be different.

"Zach, what's this?" Geena asked, looking disdainfully toward the speakers, which had just started pumping out some mellow trance music. Zach's favorite.

"My cousin totally made it on his computer," Zach said excitedly, tossing the CD case up in the air and catching it again with only a slight fumble. "It's called 'Synthetic Symphony.' Like it?"

"Yeah, it's nice," Geena said perkily. Then she wrinkled her nose and glared. "If I was in church with my aunt Maxine. Put some real music on and let's get this party started!"

While I was busy freaking out, my devoted mother was upstairs, working on a little secret project of her own. She was sitting on the edge of my bed, messing around on my laptop — but don't worry, I gave her permission. (That was my first mistake!)

"Ben, what are you doing home on a Friday night?" she called out, spotting my brother walking down the hall. "Are you feeling okay?"

"I'm gonna watch movies with Tara," he explained.

My mom got that look on her face. You know the one. It says, "My child is slowly losing his mind. What would be a nice way to tell him?"

"Honey? Tara moved to California," she reminded him as gently as she could.

He poked his head in the doorway. "We both rented scary movies and we're gonna watch 'em while we're on the phone —" He suddenly stopped himself, realizing that there was something a little strange about this picture. "Uh, Mom? Why are you in Addie's room looking at her computer?"

Unbelievable! Ben was defending my privacy? Now *that's* sticking up for your sister.

"Seeing as I'm not allowed to set foot downstairs unless someone chokes, Addie told me I could use her laptop to check my e-mail." She waved him over. "Come take a look at the e-greeting from Grandma. It's hilarious."

Ben joined Mom on the bed — probably shocked that Mom had even been able to open the e-mail in the first place. Mom and computers? Let's just say they go together about as well as peanut butter and jellyfish. But when he saw what was on the screen, he realized that he'd seriously underestimated her.

Because there on the screen, behind the e-mail, was a blurry, live-action image of . . . you guessed it, my *party*.

"My Webcam!" he exclaimed. "I thought I set that up on the computer downstairs." He looked at her suspiciously. "Why can you see it up here?"

"Oh, all the computers in the house are networked so we can monitor your online activity," Mom said cheerfully.

Um, excuse me? How does a woman who can barely use e-mail know about network spying?!

"Have you ever heard of a little thing called civil

rights?" Ben asked self-righteously — and if I'd been there, you can bet I would have been cheering him on. "What about *our* privacy?"

"It's about safety," Mom protested. "It's not like we're spying or anything."

Yeah, right. Then how come when Ben went to flick off the Webcam feed and bring up the e-mail, my mother stopped him in his tracks?

"Ooh, look at that girl Cranberry's outfit," she murmured, gazing intently at the screen. "That is *so* cute. I wonder if Addie would wear something like that. . . ."

My own mother, a *spy*? Now I know how Benedict Arnold's kid must have felt.

Guess what? The party was a success — at least it started out that way. Kids filled the room, and it actually seemed like they were having fun. All the girls were on one side of the room and the boys on the other — but it was a seventh-grade party, so what else could you expect? I'm proud to say, in fact, that it was a typical seventh-grade party in almost every way.

What? You want more detail? No problem, let's just take a little tour. Over on the boys' side, Zach and Mario were flipping through CDs. It's impossible to tear Zach away from his music.

"Then I'll put on some old school," Zach was saying. "You know, when things start to get 'fra-zeaky.'" Zach winked at Mario, and they both started laughing. I think that was about as "fra-zeaky" as either of them were going to get.

Over on the girls' side, Maris and Cranberry were hanging all over Patti Perez, who was ignoring them. (What else is new?) The three of them were a little overdressed, especially Cranberry, in her cranberry-colored gown. They looked like they'd headed out for a night on the red carpet — and instead found themselves trapped in my basement, getting their designer shoes caught in our shag carpeting.

"Let's just say, so far?" Maris said, with a disdainful flick of her fingers toward the rest of the party. "Not impressed."

"But it is early," Cranberry countered hopefully. "We might catch a glimpse of the brother."

Meanwhile, Geena was over by the snack table telling a bunch of girls about her party-food philosophy.

"As you can see," she explained, sweeping her arm out to indicate the entire spread, from corn chips to corn dogs, "the food has been carefully chosen."

The snack table was apparently the only place in the room that it was okay for guys and girls to mingle. It wasn't pretty.

"For ten bucks, would you eat all the corn dogs on that plate?" Duane Ogilvy asked some poor girl. He demonstrated his point by shoving a corn dog in his mouth. Whole. "And then afterward," he mumbled around his mouthful, "you had to, like, hold it in for two days?"

Ugh. Sometimes seventh-grade guys are just so . . . sixth grade.

Up in my bedroom, Mom was still at it. She was following the party minute by minute, her eyes glued to the screen.

"Sue, do you know where my *Canoes and Kayaks* catalog is?" my dad called from the hallway.

"It's in the bathroom where you left it," she told him. "Remember, don't flush." (Thanks, Mom — always looking out for me.)

That's when Dad poked his head into the room. "What are you doing in there?"

Mom quickly tried to shut down the program and close the laptop. "Uh, nothing," she stammered. "I'm just doing a Web search on myself. Did you know there's a Sue Singer in Idaho who collects troll dolls?"

But it was no use — she'd been caught red-handed. Dad's eyes widened when he saw what she was really looking at.

"Honey! We agreed that we would not abuse the monitoring," he chastised her. "It's wrong, sweetheart. It's deceitful. It's . . ." That's when he caught sight of me on the screen. And just like that, he was hooked. "Oh . . . look at my Addie," he gasped, sitting down on the bed next to Mom. "She's so grown-up. She's so pretty."

I know I should probably be mad that they were watching me, but come on. "Grown-up"? "Pretty"? Can I really complain about that?

"Ooh, look," Mom said, pointing enthusiastically at the screen. "Nick and Brianna are back together. She dumped him last year for an eighth grader."

"Who's that?" Dad asked, stretching out on the bed — he was obviously going to be there for a while. "These two?"

"Yeah." She nodded, and Nancy barked in agreement. What kind of world do we live in where a girl can't even trust her own dog not to spy on her?

"I'm getting kinda hungry," Dad said suddenly. "You hungry?"

Out of nowhere, Ben appeared in the doorway. Yell at him to clean up his room or to hand over the remote control, and he'll pretend he's deaf — but when it comes to the prospect of food, he's got supersonic hearing.

"I could eat."

Down in the basement, I was trying my best to relax and enjoy myself. After all, almost everything was going smoothly — even Randy Klein was having fun, body cast and all.

"Girl, wish I had a basement!" Violet Hempel said enviously as I passed her on my way to refill the hummus.

"Can I keep these old bingo numbers?" Matt Weisbein asked me as I adjusted the lighting.

Even Eli had something nice to say, for once. "Yo, Ad-die! Cool retro shag carpet."

I'd lost track of Geena for a while, but there she was, carrying out another tray of snacks. She shot me a triumphant look.

"This is just like one of those underground raves," she gushed, quickly walking past. (Geena believes in maximizing her party experience by showing herself off to as many people per minute as possible.)

And she was right. The party was a hit. *I* was a hit. Still, there was something off. Something missing. I couldn't quite put my finger on it, but . . .

"Ooh, you look so handsome in that shirt!"

"You're so funny, you should be on TV!"

I turned toward the stairs, to see what all the lame comments and high-pitched giggling was about — and there he was. Jake Behari, surrounded by a posse of stammering girls, all trying to get his attention. He saw me watching him, and before I could turn away, he smiled. And I think he was actually smiling at *me*. That's when I knew exactly what I needed to do. But would I have the nerve to do it?

It was humiliating enough that Mom, Dad, Ben, and even our dog were spending their night spying on me and my friends — but did they really have to invite the *pizza delivery guy* to watch, too? They all lay in a row, on *my* bed, following the action.

"Tara, this is way scarier than any horror movie," Ben said into the phone to his girlfriend. (I wonder if they'd set it up so that *she* could see, too.) "We did not look like that when we were thirteen."

"Did you bring those cinnamon twists we ordered?" Dad asked the pizza guy, chowing down on a heaping slice.

"That kid with the glasses has had like sixteen corn dogs," Mom observed in amazement. But no one noticed — they were too busy attacking the cinnamon twists.

So here's the situation. Jake Behari was sitting on the stairs — on *my* stairs, in *my* house. Jake Behari was in *my* house — only a few yards away. And yet I was still standing by the snack table, my feet glued to the floor. I picked up a tray of nachos — maybe I could take it over to him and his friends, ask if they wanted some. Totally casual. I could do that, right?

Wrong.

I put down the tray. No way could I just walk up to Jake Behari like we were old friends and offer him some homemade nachos. Was I crazy?

No — I was fun, fearless, and fabulous, I reminded myself. I could do this. All I had to do was smile, hold my head up high, act confident, and no one would ever know that my insides were quivering like crazy. *Okay, New and Improved Addie*, I said to myself, suddenly firm and res-olute, *let's go.*

Painting a wide grin on my face, I lifted the tray and strode across the room toward Jake. It was easier than I'd expected — just put one foot in front of the other and, step by step, I was almost —

Uh-oh.

I was trying so hard to look calm and casual that I'd forgotten all about looking where I was going. And where was I going? Straight into the stupid extension cord that Ben had strung across the room for his Webcam. My foot got caught in the cord and the rest of my body just kept going and suddenly it was up, up, and away — the nachos and I went flying through the air. Up, up, up, and then down — straight into the punch bowl. Headfirst. With a splash.

What happened after that is all a little jumbled — after all, my head was floating in punch, so I couldn't quite see or hear what was going on. But I think it's safe to say that the whole room was staring at me. I definitely heard a scream — and plenty of laughter.

As I was thrashing around in the punch, some-body finally came over to help me up. The first thing I noticed was that my look was totally ruined — my hair was sopping wet and dripping punch all over my face, and my outfit was splattered with nachos. But the second thing I noticed made me forget all about that — because the second thing was Jake Behari.

"Are you okay, Addie?" he asked, grabbing my hand and pulling me back to my feet. (Did you notice? He touched my hand — *Jake Behari* touched my hand!)

I couldn't believe it. "You . . . know my name?" I asked, stunned. (*Jake Behari* knew my name!)

"Sure." He shrugged, like it was no big deal. Little did he know. "You're in my chess class, right?"

"Oh, um, I love chess!" Maris squealed from behind him. I should have known she would have a front-row seat for my punch-bowl dive.

"Me, too!" Cranberry added. "Red and black are, like, my two favorite colors."

Jake smirked, and I suppressed a snort.

"I . . . think you're talking about checkers," he informed them, rolling his eyes in my direction. I heard Maris gasp, but I barely noticed her reaction. I was still amazed by the fact that Jake was actually talking to me. More than that, we were laughing together, as if we were on the same side. Maris and Cranberry freaking out in the background was just a little added bonus.

"So, Addie, see you in chess," Jake said, giving me a little wave and heading back off into the crowd.

I was almost too shocked to speak.

"Yeah," I finally managed to respond in a soft voice. "See ya." But he was already gone.

Geena and Zach raced up to me as soon as I was alone.

"Addie, are you all right?" Geena asked, grabbing a napkin and starting to blot my sopping-wet shirt. "I was in the kitchen when someone text-messaged me and told me what happened!"

Was I all right? I had to think about it for a moment — after all, I was covered in fruit punch and nachos, and I'd just made a fool of myself in front of my whole grade. Again. It looked like I would be "Nachorina" or "Puncherella" for the rest of the year.

But then I smiled and nodded.

"I'm fine," I assured her. And I was amazed to discover that it was true. In fact, more than fine. "*Great,* actually."

Zach shrugged in confusion, ready to move on. "Good, then you won't mind asking your dad to go on a nacho run." He gestured to my ruined shirt, covered in spatters of cheese and salsa. "You're wearing our last batch."

I nodded, barely listening to him. I was too busy thinking over what had just happened. Zach was clueless — but Geena saw the glint in my eye. She knew.

"Two words," she whispered, leaning close and offering me a knowing smile. "Jake. Behari."

Exactly.

*   *   *

So now you know what I mean when I say that things don't always end up the way you expect them to. And as it turns out, sometimes that's for the best. I mean, the party was totally fun. Patti Perez almost fainted when Ben ran down to make sure no punch spilled on his Webcam. Plus, my family owed me huge for spying — and for getting pizza crumbs in my bed.

For the whole week after my party, they were at my beck and call. I had Ben doing my laundry, Nancy running errands for me, and Mom and Dad bringing me milk and cookies on a daily basis. What a life.

As for the whole New and Improved Addie thing, well . . . so it turns out that some things haven't changed as much as I thought. I'm still a giant klutz, destined to make a fool out of myself again and again. But you know what? Maybe that's okay. After all, I've got my friends, my family, and *myself*. And besides, Jake Behari knows my name — how much better can it get? It's like my new song says:

> *You can't always be fabulous*
> *Or in control.*
> *Sometimes you've just gotta roll with the punches*
> *Or in the punch bowl.*
> *I can handle a few new names.*

I'm a Punch Rocker, Puncherella, Punch Master,
Peter Punchkinhead, Punchy Magee,
Addie the Punchface Girl,
So punch in your Karaoke
for Princess Punchanoke
Ya better get to know me
'cause I pack a mean punch.
I'm a Punch Rocker . . . I'm a Punch Rocker, oh, yeah,
I'm a Punch Rocker!
I'm a Punch, Punch, Punch, Punch Rocker!

Of course, just when you think you've got every-thing figured out, seventh grade is there to remind you just how wrong you are. For a few weeks after the big party, everything went okay. You know how it is at the start of a new school year. At first you're totally stressed, trying to memorize your new schedule and your new locker combination, and trying to figure out which teach-ers are friendly and which will give you detention for sneezing.

And then there are those other days, the ones where your world turns upside down — and all you want is to get back to normal, but you're not sure how.

This was about to be one of those days.

We were sitting in social studies, listening to Mr. Ward explain the new class project. Mr. Ward is one of those teachers who still thinks he can make a difference and mold our young minds. He's cheerful, friendly, and superenthusiastic — which is great, except when he comes up with yet another of his "fun" class projects.

"So, you will be paired up and assigned famous duos from history to portray in a presentation for class on Friday," he explained. "This is your chance to make history come alive!"

Lucky us. Geena, who was sitting behind me, leaned forward to whisper, "This always happens. Teachers get bored with their own lives and force you to dress up like trained seals for their amusement." She rolled her eyes. "So sad."

I couldn't agree more. Mr. Ward, however, was another story.

"Ms. Fabiano?" he asked, casting a knowing look in our direction. "Do you have something to share with the rest of the class?"

"You mean besides my winning smile and personality?" Standing up, Geena flashed a grin and batted her eyes at him — he didn't crack a smile. So she tried another tack.

"Uh . . . Addie and I want to be partners," she said, quickly sitting down again.

Don't you love how she ropes me into these things?

"Okay," Mr. Ward agreed. "Geena and Addie — Jefferson and Ross." Then he pointed to Zach and his friend Freddy. "Zach and Freddy — Dr. King and Rosa Parks."

Zach thumped his chest with pride — he likes to think of himself as a young Martin Luther King Jr., campaigning for freedom and justice. At least *someone* was excited about this project.

"Maris and Cranberry..." Mr. Ward continued, pausing to think. "...I was thinking John D. Rockefeller and J. P. Morgan."

"Who?" they chorused in confusion.

Lucky for them, Zach had actually done his reading.

"Alleged 'captains of industry' who rose to financial success on the broken backs of American factory workers," he explained, looking pretty impressed with himself.

Maris's and Cranberry's faces were as blank as an empty sheet of paper.

Zach noticed their expressions and shook his head, realizing he would need to dumb things down a bit. "Two old rich dudes," Zach clarified.

"Score!" they said together, their faces lighting up in anticipation.

As they exchanged high fives, Geena and I exchanged our second eye roll of the morning. And it was only Monday. . . .

The whole dress-up idea didn't seem any more appealing after Mr. Ward explained all the details. After class, we couldn't stop talking about how stupid it was. Or at least, *I* couldn't stop.

"Have you guys ever heard of a lamer assignment?" I asked Geena and Zach as we were walking down the hall toward our lockers.

Zach just shrugged, and Geena ignored me. She was thumbing through our history book looking for info on her character. Suddenly, she slammed it shut and looked up at me in horror.

"Oh, no!" she gasped in horror. "*Betsy* Ross? I thought he meant *Diana* Ross."

I was about to point out that in some ways, Betsy Ross was like our country's first fashion designer, but I got a little . . . distracted. I couldn't help it. Jake Behari walked right by us — and as he passed me, he smiled.

"Hey, Addie," he said as he strolled down the hall. He was wearing a maroon T-shirt that totally set off his deep tan, and the way he had his backpack slung over one shoulder? It was just so . . . cool. Sigh. I hoped I wasn't blushing too obviously. Could Jake Behari be any more perfect?

I opened my mouth to say something back to him, but no words came out. So instead I just twisted around and watched him saunter away. I loved to watch the way his shiny, shaggy brown hair bounced with his swaying walk.

Geena had, of course, missed the whole encounter. She was still obsessing over our history project.

"Look at her!" she complained, opening up the book again and pointing at an ugly painting of Betsy Ross. "She looks like Orville Redenbacher."

Um, can we focus on what's *really* important here?

"You guys, Jake Behari just said hi to me," I pointed out. "Do you think he likes me?"

I waited and waited for them to answer, my heart filled with fear. But after a moment, they both smiled widely.

"Oh, totally," Geena said.

"You are so *in*," Zach agreed.

And as soon as they said it, I wanted to dance down the hallway, to sing at the top of my lungs. I felt like I could fly. *Jake Behari* liked *me*. It was unbelievable.

Now, I know what you're thinking. Not so fast, Addie. Maybe your friends are just telling you what you want to hear, Addie. But you don't understand — not my friends. No way. We always told one another the real deal.

I can always counts on Geena and Zach, my best friends in the entire world, to tell me the truth, the whole truth, and nothing but the truth. They're always totally honest with me. Like last year, when we all had to make posters to celebrate Dental Health Week.

"Do you guys think my Dental Health poster's the best?" I asked them, proudly holding up my drawing of a giant mouth. *"I do. I'm really good at drawing the teeth."*
They nodded enthusiastically.
"Totally!" Zach cheered.
"You're so gonna win first place," Geena said confidently.

They're always in my corner — and that's how I know I can believe in whatever they say.

"Anyway, I'm just going to have to do some revisionist history," Geena decided, still worrying about her Betsy Ross makeover. "If anyone can glam up Betsy Ross, it's me, right?"

"Just don't try and make her skirt out of plastic

wrap like you did for the Christmas pageant," I warned her, laughing.

"Oh, man. You got detention for six weeks for that," Zach remembered with a grin. "That was so funny."

Suddenly, our walk down the hall turned into a trip down memory lane.

"Not half as funny as when you tried to protest that pizza place they were building on protected swampland," Geena countered, shaking her head at the thought of it.

"Yeah, you chained yourself to the Porta Potti and threw up because it smelled so bad," I reminded him. Geena and I couldn't stop giggling at the memory.

"How about that time Addie wrote that awful song when she thought her dog, Nancy, ran away?" Geena asked.

Uh . . . what?

"But it turns out she was just hiding in the laundry basket," Zach said, gasping with laughter. He started fake playing a guitar and singing. *My* song. *"Laundry dog, laundry dog, don't let the Tide take her away. HOWWWWWWL."*

"That was hysterical, Addie," Geena said — and only then did she realize that I was no longer walking with them. I'd stopped, frozen in the middle of the hallway, stunned. *These* were my two best friends in the world? The ones I could trust to *always* be on my side and *always* tell me the truth? Something was seriously wrong here.

"You guys said you loved that song," I said, backing away from them.

"Come on," Geena protested, squirming under my accusing gaze. "We can't love *every* song you write."

Well, I don't see why not. But that wasn't even the point.

"I know that," I told her, crossing my arms in anger. "But why did you lie and tell me you liked it when you didn't?"

"Well, 'lied' is such a strong word," Geena hedged. She looked at Zach for support, and I waited to see what he could say that would make things better.

"We were just trying to be nice," Zach claimed.

Sorry, that wasn't it.

"I can't believe it," I exclaimed. "This is the first time you guys have lied to me."

There was a long pause. A long, guilty pause. Geena and Zach exchanged a glance . . . and suddenly, I had a feeling I wasn't going to like what came next.

"Well . . ." Geena looked up, down, sideways, any-where but directly at me. "It's not the *first* time. Remember Dental Health Week?"

"Do you guys think my Dental Health poster's the best? I do. I'm really good at drawing the teeth."
"Totally!" Zach cheered.
"You're so gonna win first place," Geena assured me.

Okay, so that part sounded familiar enough. But then she kept going.

"Right after I win the lottery," Zach muttered to Geena as they walked off down the hall a step behind me.
Geena gave the poster another once-over and shook her head in disgust. *"And I become the Queen of England,"* she whispered back.
And then they laughed.

Laughed. At *me*! And they'd done it behind my back. That was the worst part, I realized. So what if they didn't have the taste to appreciate what I'd drawn (a giant mouth on little stick legs)? That wasn't the point.

The point was, I'd *trusted* them to give me their *honest* opinion. And what had they done instead?

"You guys lied to me about my Dental Health poster?" I asked incredulously. They both looked totally sheepish and apologetic, but it was too late for excuses.

"Well, you were so excited about it," Zach explained. "We just didn't want to hurt your feelings."

"Besides, things like that," Geena added, "they're not exactly lies."

"They're *not* truths, either," I pointed out. I couldn't believe I had to explain the difference to her, of all people. But she still wasn't getting it.

"I guess they're somewhere in between," Geena offered, trying for a compromise.

"I like to think of them as *luths*," Zach suggested. Then his face brightened. "Hey, new word! I gotta add that to my slang-tionary."

I had a new word for his slang-tionary, too.

Bestuddled. It's a combination of betrayed, stunned, and befuddled — the way you feel when you discover that your best friends in the world are big, fat liars.

That night, as I helped my mom get ready for dinner, I told her all about what had happened. I don't think she quite got the point of the story.

"I mean, who knows if anything they've ever told me is true," I griped.

"Well, that's horrible," Mom agreed, washing some lettuce in the sink.

"I know, I thought they were —"

That's when she held up her finger, the universal sign for "hold that thought." And I realized she wasn't listening to me at all — she was talking to a client on her headset phone. My mother's a real estate agent, which means she sometimes has to work weird hours. That's okay, usually — but not when I'm in the middle of a Major Crisis.

"They're going to have to go at least five thousand over the asking price even to be in the running," she said into the phone. "Well, it's a sellers' market. Can you check on the chicken?"

I was still stewing about Zach and Geena.

"Addie, chicken?" Mom repeated, putting a hand over the mouthpiece of her headset and giving me an expectant look.

Oh, that was meant for me?

I sighed, and opened the oven door, using a pot holder to pull out a casserole dish full of chicken breasts. Careful not to drop it, I laid the dish on top of the stove. Did that count as "checking the chicken"? Who knew?

Ben walked into the kitchen and started to grab a piece of lettuce out of Mom's colander.

"Don't pick," she chided him, slapping his hand away. "That's barbaric. No, not you," she added into the mouthpiece. "I mean, yes, you're going to have to pick a buyer eventually. . . ."

"What's for dinner?" Ben asked me. We sat down at the kitchen table together, staring down at our empty plates. Have I mentioned that food is all Ben ever thinks about? Other than his girlfriend, Tara, of course. And actually, that gave me an idea. . . .

"Either chicken casserole or a sunny two-bedroom loft. I can't quite tell. Ben —"

"I should get one of those headsets to talk to

Tara," he mused, ignoring me and staring off in Mom's direction with a dreamy expression. "Then I could do curls with both hands." He began pumping imaginary weights, considering the idea. Hard as it was not to mock him, I decided that this time, I needed information more than I needed a good laugh.

"Ben, has Tara ever lied to you?" I asked.

"She's my girlfriend," he reminded me, snorting at the idea. "Of course not."

"Not even nice polite white lies?" I pressed him. "Like 'nice haircut' or 'I like your Dental Health poster'? to choose a totally random example."

Ben shook his head and adopted his best "wise big brother" tone. "Addie, Addie, Addie." He put his hand on my shoulder and gave me a shake for each time he said my name. He was *really* lucky I needed his help.

"Honesty is the key to any relationship," he said sadly, as if pitying that I had yet to grasp such a crucial concept. Ben's only a couple years older than me, but sometimes he acts like he's the wisest man on earth and I have all the life experience of a tadpole. "It's like an unspoken contract. If Tara tells me that she likes my Dental Health poster, then she likes my Dental Health poster." He paused, then looked up at me in alarm. "Why, what have you heard?"

71

Before I could pump him for more information, Dad breezed into the kitchen, tossing his keys on the counter and rushing over to us.

"Sorry I'm late," he apologized, knowing how much Mom hates it when he misses dinner. "I know, I know, but an entire Little League team came into the store at ten minutes to closing. I was up to my eyeballs in —"

He stopped suddenly and stared at the kitchen table — fully set, but with no food in sight.

"Was it my night to pick up dinner?" he asked in confusion.

Mom brought over the tray of chicken casserole and a heaping bowl of salad, laying them down on the table in front of us.

"Honey, it hasn't been your night to pick up dinner since you ripped the label off an old ketchup bottle and told us it was marinara sauce," she reminded him fondly.

Ugh. Some memories are best forgotten.

"Ah, yes," Dad said, nodding. "Addie still gags when you say the word *spaghetti*."

Ech. Blech. Yech. Ugh. I'll never be able to look at a plate of pasta the same way again.

Can you blame me?

"Anyway," Dad continued, serving himself a giant

serving of casserole, "it's starting to be the busy season at the store, so I think it's about time Ben comes in and helps out his old dad." He gave Ben an affectionate whack on the shoulder. "You start Monday, kiddo."

Ben looked down and started playing with his food. "Ohhh, um . . . "

Dad squinted at him, then grinned. "Okay, you drive a hard bargain. How does a fifty-cents-an-hour raise from last year sound?"

"Yeah, uh . . ." Ben looked at me, looked at Mom, then finally met Dad's eyes and gave him a rueful smile. "The thing is, between wrestling, and school, and talking to Tara on the phone . . . I just don't have time for a job this year."

There was a long silence, and we all stared at Dad, waiting to see how he would take the news.

"Oh, of course you don't," he eventually assured Ben, nodding. "School, wrestling, and your long-distance relationship come first." It sounded almost like he was trying to convince himself. "I guess I can always hire someone else."

Ben sighed in obvious relief and slapped him on the back.

"Thanks for understanding, Dad," he said heartily.

"No problem," Dad said quietly. "I appreciate the honesty."

Now, you see that? Is it that hard for people to just be open and honest with each other? Look how well it works when you tell the whole truth! If only there was some way that I could make Zach and Geena understand. . . .

I thought about it long and hard, and late that night, I finally came up with a brilliant idea. (I hate to admit it, but it actually came from Ben and that "unspoken contract" thing he has with Tara.) The next day, we'd make a fresh start. A totally *honest* start. It's like my new song says:

> *Geena and Zach don't have my back.*
> *I thought we were friends, but the lies gotta end.*
> *H. O. N. E. S. T. Y. Honesty's the thing to live by.*
> *H. O. N. S. T. Y. I forgot the "E,"*
> *but I can't forget the lies.*

The next day after school, I met Geena and Zach at *Juice!*, our favorite hangout. *Juice!* is a juice bar (I know, big surprise). But it's not just any juice bar. From the candy-colored tables to the graffiti-style *Juice!* logo on all the walls, it's a fun, laid-back place to hang. There's always awesome music bursting from the speakers — and they have 101 flavors of juice, including my favorite, Strawberry Blastoff.

When I got there, Geena and Zach were already sitting down. Perfect. I stalked over to them and slammed a piece of paper down on their table.

"What is this?" Geena asked, looking up at me in confusion.

"It's an 'Honesty Is the Best Policy' policy," I explained. I'd stayed up for hours the night before getting the wording exactly right. Zach read it aloud:

"'We the undersigned, Geena Fabiano, Zach Carter-Schwartz, and Addie Singer, do hereby swear to henceforth be totally honest with one another.'"

I handed the contract to Geena so that she could take a closer look.

"From the moment we sign it, we agree to be a hundred percent, totally and completely honest with one another," I informed them. "An end to all the lies."

"Luths," Zach corrected me.

"Those, too," I allowed.

Geena read through the policy, then shrugged.

"Okay," she agreed, digging her favorite hot-pink fuzzy-headed pen out of her bag. "Honestly? I think this idea is stupid, but you're my friend, so I'll agree to sign it."

"Great!" I said. It was working already.

Geena signed and handed the paper over to Zach.

"Can I have a different pen?" he asked, viewing the pink fuzz with distrust.

The answer was no — so finally he gave in and signed, too.

"This is perfect!" I said excitedly, sitting down with them. "And since we're being honest, Zach, you have a blackberry seed in your tooth."

After all, I had to set a good example, didn't I?

With a look of panic, Zach grabbed the large shiny pendant hanging around Geena's neck and twisted his head so he could see his teeth in the reflection. He started digging around in his mouth with his fingernail, which was so disgusting, I was grateful when Geena abruptly pulled away.

"Wait a minute," Geena pointed out suspiciously. "You're drinking a Mocha Moo Cow, 'all dairy, no berry.'"

Zach blushed and rubbed the back of his neck. "Ah . . . well . . ." he stammered, stalling for time. "I told you the busboy cleared your Berry-ma-taz smoothie when you went to the bathroom, but the truth is, I chugged it," he admitted. "And it was goooooood." He looked kind of ashamed — but then, suddenly, a grin lit up his face. "Wow, that was easy."

"See?" I crowed. This whole honesty thing was going to be even better than I'd expected.

And speaking of honesty, I suddenly heard a *very* familiar voice drifting over from the counter.

"Duane, your Orange-tastic with energy boost is ready."

Wait a second . . . I knew that voice.

I looked over to the counter, only to see *Ben*, decked out in a purple *Juice!* T-shirt and bright orange *Juice!* cap. He was handing a cup of juice over to Duane, the skinny geek from my chess class, and ringing up his purchase. All the evidence pointed to one thing: Ben was working at *Juice!* But that couldn't be. Ben didn't have time for a job, remember? I'd been sitting right there at the kitchen table when he'd explained it. *Apparently*, he needed some reminding. And I was just the sister to do it.

I strode over to the counter, passing by Duane, who was clutching his Orange-tastic smoothie like his life depended on it.

"I'm on day twelve of a seventy-two-week juice cleanse," Duane explained. But I didn't have time to hear about his freakish diet. First I had to deal with the freak I was related to.

"Ben? What are you doing here?" I asked righteously. "You told Dad that —"

"Addie, let me try and explain this to you," Ben said patronizingly, looking up from the cash register. "There comes a time when a boy has to step out from underneath his father's shadow and prove to the world that he's his own man. *Capisce?*"

He picked up the tip jar and shook it at me, and it only took me a moment to realize what he was getting at. See, ever since Ben's bar mitzvah, he tries to turn everything into a rite of passage, hoping people will give him money. But if he thought I was going to reward him for lying to Dad? He was even denser than I'd thought.

"Look, at Dad's store, I'm stuck selling bathing suits to sweaty old guys," Ben continued, when it became obvious I wasn't going anywhere near his tip jar. "Here, I'm out in the open, free to chat up all the cute girls." Hmm, I wondered how that figured into Ben and Tara's "unspoken contract."

We both took a moment to look around the café at all the "cute girls." By which I mean: me, Geena, and one woman who looked like she'd just celebrated her ninety-ninth birthday. She looked up from her knitting to give Ben a coy smile and a flirty wave. Sure, I could see exactly what he was talking about — here at *Juice!* he was sur-rounded by hotties.

"They just haven't come in yet," he said defensively, noticing my skeptical look. "You can't tell Dad," he pleaded.

"You want me to *lie* to him?" I asked incredulously.

He nodded vigorously. "Yeah, that would be great. Hey, tell him I was at wrestling this afternoon."

"That's not what I meant," I snapped. Didn't he realize that I was campaigning for truth? What happened to the "unspoken contract"? Apparently, that didn't apply to Ben and my dad, but I wasn't about to get involved.

"It's no big deal," Ben cajoled me, in that smooth-talker tone he usually reserves for Tara. "Come on. Geena and Zach have had the decency to keep this a secret for me. And they're not even my sister."

Geena and Zach have —

I spun around to face my two best friends. *More* lies? Were they kidding me with this?

"You guys knew he was working here?" I asked, outraged. "And you didn't tell me."

They just shrugged.

"He asked us not to say anything," Geena claimed, shooting Ben a "you blew it" glare.

"But I'm your best friend," I pointed out. I peered

at them both intently, wondering what other secrets lay behind those innocent-looking faces. "Anything else you've been keeping from me, Geena . . . if that is your *real* name?"

Geena raised an eyebrow. "Well, since you asked — that sweatshirt is way too small for you."

I looked down at myself. I was wearing a light blue hooded sweatshirt, with VARSITY written across it in light pink cursive lettering. I'd had it for years, and it was one of my favorites. And yeah, *maybe* it was a little tight, and maybe the sleeves ended a few inches above my wrists, but that didn't necessarily mean it was too small. Did it? No way — Geena was totally wrong.

"She's right!" Zach agreed. "Wow, this honesty thing is so freeing."

I gave them a weak smile and sat back down at the table across from my two so-called best friends. They both beamed at me, as if to say, "Congratulations, you finally got exactly what you wanted."

And, uh, yeah . . . I guess I did.

After that last "luth" about Ben, I decided that it was time for us to get it all out. No more lies, luths, or anything. Zach and Geena agreed to come over later that week for an "honesty spill." I figured all we had to do was admit to all the past lies, then we could start with a clean slate. We shut ourselves up in my bedroom and sat in a circle on the floor, back to back. That part was Geena's idea. She said that way, it would be less intimidating, like how no one looks at the priest during confession.

"So, who starts?" Zach asked.

"I'll go first," Geena volunteered. She took a deep breath. "Addie, remember when I borrowed your yellow sweater and I told you I was attacked by moths?"

"Yeah." I frowned at the memory. Such a shame. That had been my favorite sweater.

"Truth is, I spilled hot chocolate all over it, so I gave it to Nancy to eat the evidence."

What? The *dog* ate my favorite sweater? I bit my lip and counted to ten, trying to stay calm. This truth stuff was harder than it looked. But if Geena could do it . . .

"Um, okay," I mumbled, my mind racing for something I could admit. "Remember when I wrote that song 'Maris Is an Ugly Troll'? And you guys asked if I'd ever written any mean songs about you and I said no. . . . Well . . ."

I grabbed my guitar and, with just a hint of doubt, began playing one of my old masterpieces, "Zack Is Whack."

"Zach is so stubborn, he drives me crazy. / He only holds sit-ins 'cause he's too darn lazy / to stand."

I stopped after a couple of lines, glad that I couldn't see the look on Zach's face. "It doesn't mean anything," I assured him. "They're just . . . a healthy way to vent."

"They?" Zach asked, his voice cracking. "How many other mean songs have you written about me?"

Well, we'd promised one another nothing but the truth, right? I got up and pawed through my bookshelf, digging out my collection of Zach songs. It was a giant three-ring binder, about six inches thick, bursting with pages of song lyrics. I tossed it on the floor next to him, where it landed with a loud thud.

"Um, do I have a binder, too?" Geena asked hesitantly.

"Not exactly a binder . . ." I began, giggling at the memory of the day Ben had opened up the hall closet, looking for his in-line skates, and had gotten buried by an avalanche of Geena lyrics.

"So, anyway," I said quickly, deciding it was time to change the subject, "remember when I told Geena I liked the dress she wore to Zach's Arbor Day party? Well, honestly, I thought it was a little . . . risqué. Zach?"

"I hate it when Addie uses pseudo-French words like 'risqué.'"

From there on in, the confessions came fast and furious.

Oh, *really*? "I told Geena I was sick the night of her mall fashion show," I shot back, "but I really went to watch Jake's soccer match."

"That's almost as gross as the time I told Addie the bug in her soup was a mushroom chunk 'cause I didn't want to wait in the cafeteria line again," Geena revealed rather fearlessly.

"Ugh!" I cried. "You made me eat a bug?!" I could

almost feel it crawling around in my mouth and started spitting to try to get rid of the imaginary buggy taste. It didn't work. "Blech! Ptooie! Why did you tell me that?!"

"You're the one who wanted us to be honest," Zach pointed out.

Yes, honest — not mean, spiteful, and totally gross.

"I think we're finished here," I said coolly, standing up.

Geena and Zach both rose from the floor, without a word to me or to each other. Once they'd finished pushing each other out of the way in an attempt to get out of the door first, they both walked out. And didn't look back.

Looks like our "honesty spill" had turned into a toxic waste dump.

"Can you believe it, Mom?" I complained that night. "They lied to me."

I was standing on a little platform in the basement, trying to stay still as my mom hemmed the bottom of my Thomas Jefferson knickers.

"Addie, Geena and Zach are your best friends," she reminded me, clenching a bunch of straight pins between her teeth. "We all tell little white lies sometimes."

Funny, that's not what she told me last summer,

when I lied about having cleaned my room so that I could go out for ice cream and got grounded for a week.

"So what makes some lies okay and some not?" I asked, confused.

"It's hard to say," she hedged. "You have to trust your gut. Now, hold still before I stick a pin through Thomas Jefferson's calf."

I tried my best, but when Ben walked past with a wad of dirty clothes and a bottle of dish soap, I almost fell off my box. Ben? Actually doing a chore? Voluntarily?

"I'm gonna do some laundry real quick," he muttered, trying to speed past us toward the washing machine.

"With dish soap?" I asked pointedly.

"Yes, with dish soap," he retorted, as if it were the most natural thing in the world. He scoured the label, looking for a way to explain himself. "It's got aloe and lanolin in it."

"Ben, why don't you just leave it," Mom suggested. You could tell she was trying her best not to laugh — it wasn't working too well. "I'll stick it in with my next load."

Ben ignored the suggestion and set his load down on top of the washing machine.

"Mom, there comes a time when a boy has to get out from underneath his mother's shadow —"

"Oh, for the love of Pete, I'm not going to pay you for doing your own laundry." She rolled her eyes and got up to grab the laundry away from him, but he held on tight. Now *this* was getting interesting. For a minute, there was a tug-of-war between them, with the wad of laundry serving as a rope.

"Honey, I've got it, just —"

"No, I'll do it myself —"

"Give it to me and —"

"No, I —"

Back and forth, back and forth, and then suddenly, the laundry all fell to the ground in a messy heap.

Mom bent down to start picking up the pile, and when she stood up again, I understood what all the fuss was about.

"*Juice!*?" she asked, dangling Ben's new uniform in front of him.

He chewed on the edge of his lip. "Uh, would you buy 'Everyone's wearing them now'?"

I shook my head. That was feeble, even for Ben.

"You're working at *Juice!*?" Mom said, ignoring him. "Why didn't you tell us?"

"He didn't want to hurt Dad's feelings," I put in, figuring it couldn't hurt to speak up in his defense. Wrong again.

"Addie!" she exclaimed, turning on me. "You knew about this?"

"Uh . . . white lie, Mom," I pointed out. "Remember?"

Ben took the uniform back from Mom and gave her a hangdog look. "You're not going to tell Dad about this, are you?" he begged.

Mom shook her head. "Of course not." Ben sagged in relief — but only for a second, because then she spoke again. "You are."

I didn't speak to Geena and Zach again that night. As far as I was concerned, I would have been happy to never speak to them again. There was just one little problem with that. The next day was Friday, the day of our social studies presentations, and Geena and I were still partners.

That morning I stepped into the classroom and spotted Betsy Ross standing by her desk, holding a tray of pies.

"Geena," I said coolly.

She gave me a terse nod. "Addie."

"I like your costume," I said grudgingly. I had to admit, it was a spectacular ensemble — Geena had definitely managed to glam up Betsy Ross. She was decked out entirely in red, white, and blue, from the American flag bonnet atop her giant blond wig to the star-spangled miniskirt. I was certain the Founding Fathers had never seen anything like it.

"I like yours," Geena echoed. I was dressed somewhat more conservatively, in one of my father's old suit jackets and the knickers my mother had made. I had a wig of my own (apparently, back then, *everyone* wore wigs), and a three-cornered hat. Just like the real Thomas Jefferson.

I gave Geena a tight smile. So far, so good. Maybe we could make it through this presentation together without a major blowup. Still, I felt like we were walking on a tightrope together. One wrong move and . . .

"I see you remembered the Boston cream pies," I commented, gesturing at her tray.

She nodded proudly. "Yes. Representing the Boston Tea Party, the catalyst for the American Revolution. I made them myself."

"Really." My lips curled up in a fake smile. "I hope there are no bugs in them."

"Funny," Geena replied. But she didn't look like she'd be laughing any time soon. "Why don't you just write a song about it?"

Who knows what we would have said next if Mr. Ward hadn't started the class.

"Okay, if we're ready," he said, clearing his throat and waiting for us all to quiet down. "Ladies and gentlemen, I take you back to the Revolutionary War." He grinned at us and ushered us up to the front of the room, obviously eager to see what we'd come up with. Little did he know what he was getting himself into.

Geena and I stood up next to each other in front of the class.

"The Revolutionary War was a period of both great turmoil and great progress in America's history," Geena began.

"Mostly because Thomas Jefferson, *unlike* Betsy Ross, always believed in being honest and not basing entire friendships on *lies*," I added, shooting Geena a nasty look. What? I couldn't help myself, okay?

As the class let out a hushed gasp in the background, Geena threw down her poster board in anger and turned on me. I took a step back. Angry Geena isn't a pretty sight.

"Let us not forget about the pivotal moment in history," Geena said loudly, pointing an accusing finger in my direction, "when Thomas Jefferson called Jake Behari, pretending to be taking a 'Who's hot?' poll."

Total betrayal! I could feel my face getting red as the anger rose within me.

"Well — maybe if Betsy Ross had come to Thomas Jefferson's sleepover, that might not have happened," I snapped.

"Oh, it's on now," Freddy piped up in the background, getting ready to witness an all-out fight, but Geena ignored him.

"I'd be curious to hear what Martin Luther King has to say about that," she said, turning her fierce gaze on Zach, "since he was the one forced to let you braid his hair!"

"Hey! Leave me out of this!" Zach protested. He stood up and gave us his best Martin Luther King impression. "I maintain a strict policy of nonviolence!"

Mr. Ward stepped forward to cut us off. Apparently, he'd expected us to *talk* about the war, not act out its sequel.

"Okay, okay," he said loudly, "that was a . . . riveting project, but I think it's time to see what J. P. Morgan and Rockefeller have to say."

I slouched down in my seat, sulking. Not that I wasn't glad Mr. Ward had put us out of our misery, but I was still fuming about all the things Geena had said, and the last thing I wanted to do was sit through a Maris and Cranberry production.

Although it looked like I wouldn't have to.

When the two girls stood up, I realized that, unlike the rest of us, who looked like rejects from the annual Halloween parade, they were still wearing regular clothes.

"In the spirit of portraying filthy rich people who can buy and sell anyone," Cranberry explained, "we've taken the liberty of hiring sixth graders to do our presentation."

Maris snapped her fingers, and at her signal, two sixth graders bounded into the room, wearing suits, white wigs, and monocles. They both looked like little businessmen — and they were both obviously scared to death of Maris. Mr. Ward looked horrified.

"And maybe if Geena's lucky, she'll land herself a rich husband," Maris added. She and Cranberry did their lame finger tap in place of a high five. "Burn!" they jeered together.

"That wasn't a burn," Geena protested. "It didn't even make sense."

"Shut it, Butt-sy Ross," Maris retorted.

"Now *that* was a burn," Zach observed, sticking his nose in where it didn't belong. Zach was always doing that, I realized, my anger bubbling over.

"I thought you wanted to stay out of it, King!" I exclaimed, pulling off my Thomas Jefferson hat and flinging it toward him. I had perfect aim. Just one problem. Zach ducked.

And the hat hit Maris squarely in the face. Bull's-eye — literally.

"My eye!" Maris cried, freaking out and clutching her head. "Is my makeup okay?"

"Okay, maybe we should wrap this up —" Mr. Ward said ineffectually.

But I just talked over him. "Maybe the honest truth is that Betsy Ross was a lousy friend," I yelled, "and Thomas Jefferson shouldn't trust a single word she ever says again!"

"Oh, yeah?" Geena asked. Yeah — and what was she going to do about it?

I was about to find out.

"Eat pie, Jefferson!" Geena grabbed one of her pies off the tray and hurled it toward me. I ducked just in time — and the pie slammed Zach, covering him in Boston cream.

"So much for nonviolence," Zach sputtered, spitting out a mouthful of cream. He grabbed a pie of his own and, before I realized what was happening, threw it in my direction.

Splat!

Have you ever had a faceful of Boston cream pie? It's like getting covered with slime. And I knew someone who had yet to experience the joy. . . .

I grabbed Geena by the lapel with one hand and a pie with the other. Then I shoved the pie into her face.

Splurch!

A close-range hit.

"This is quite enough," Mr. Ward interjected, foolishly stepping into the middle of the action. "There is no need to reenact the American Revolution with Boston cream —"

WHAM!

"— pies," Mr. Ward finished, a mask of pie cream dripping down his face and spattering onto his blue shirt.

That was pretty much the end of our presentations.

Unfortunately, I suspected, it might also be the end of us.

Zach, Geena, and I all slumped in seats in the waiting room outside the principal's office, waiting for it to be our turn to face the firing squad. We sat in a row against the wall and stared straight ahead. We hadn't spoken since Mr. Ward dragged us down here. With our period costumes and spattered faces, we must have looked like we'd been involved in some bizarre, turn-of-the-century cream-puff incident. I guess we should have been happy for the delay — but I couldn't feel too relieved. After all, we were only waiting because Principal Brandywine was in there with my parents.

"Never in all my years as principal of this fine institution have I witnessed such barbaric behavior!" I could hear her yelling from behind the door. "Addie and her friends have turned icons of our proud American history into pie-throwing buffoons."

I stifled a giggle — Principal Brandywine sure did have a way with words — and when I snuck a glance over at Geena and Zach, I realized they were doing the same. We exchanged a quick smile, but then quickly looked away again.

"This is a place of learning," Principal Brandywine's voice continued. "Not the mosh pit at Punk Palace."

I couldn't hold it in anymore. I burst into laughter. At the exact same moment, so did Zach and Geena. For a few seconds, laughing with one another, it was like old times again. Somehow, Principal Brandywine had managed to bring us together. Maybe somehow, things could actually get back to normal?

"Man," Geena choked out, trying to catch her breath, "I can't wait to hear the song you're gonna write about this one."

I smiled at the thought of it — I already had some lyrics floating around in my head. "But ... you have to tell me if you don't like it this time," I insisted.

"I'm sorry we lied about stuff," she finally said, tucking a cream-soaked tendril of hair back under her wig.

"That honesty contract was so stupid," I admitted. "Let's just never talk about it again."

"That might not be a problem," Geena said ruefully. "If I get in too much trouble, my mom's gonna send me to Catholic school. I'll be too busy repenting to talk about anything."

Zach and I burst into laughter again at Geena's joke — and then we realized that she hadn't even cracked a smile.

"I'm not kidding," Geena told us, pursing her lips and looking distressed. "One more serious infringement and it's nothing but nuns and plaid jumpers from here on out."

Before I could think of something comforting to say, the door of the principal's office swung open, and my parents appeared in the doorway.

"I assure you," Dad told Principal Brandywine on his way out, "we do not encourage this style of nonverbal communication in the home."

"And we never eat pie," Mom maintained weakly. "We don't even have dessert most nights."

Principal Brandywine waved them away. On their way out, Dad stopped and stared down at me, shooting me a disappointed look.

"We will talk about this tonight, young lady," he said sternly. He and Mom shook their heads and then walked off down the hall. Now there was just one thing left to do: Face Principal Brandywine. She stormed out of her office and stood in front of us, hands on her hips.

"All right," she said, staring us down like a police inspector. "I'm ready for the three of you now. I want you to be honest and tell me: *Who* threw the first pie?"

I snuck a glance at Zach. Zach looked over at Geena. Geena looked back at me. None of us knew what to do. It's not like either Zach or I wanted to rat out Geena — and Geena certainly didn't want to get sent to Catholic school. Maybe if we just played dumb —

"Or perhaps you'd like to maintain your silence," Principal Brandywine continued, when it became clear that no one was stepping forward. She started waving a finger at us, her voice getting louder and angrier with every word. "If you do, I'll suspend all three of you until this situation can be —"

"Wait," Geena cut in, starting to rise from her chair. "It was — ow!"

I grabbed her wrist and pulled her down again, then stood up myself and faced the principal.

"It was *me*," I told Principal Brandywine. Maybe the truth isn't always the best policy. I mean, I couldn't let Geena get shipped off to a convent. And if you think about it, maybe it was kind of the truth, maybe I *was* the one who had started this whole thing. After all, the honesty contract was my stupid idea — and if it hadn't been for that, none of us would be here, covered in pie and facing suspension.

Geena shot me a look of gratitude, and for a second, I felt pretty good about myself. That is, until I turned back to Principal Brandywine and saw the gleam in her eyes. I could tell she'd already dreamed up a punishment for us . . . and I didn't think we were going to like it.

"And wipe those smiles off your faces," she snapped as we trooped into her office, single file. She slammed the door behind us — it sounded like a prison gate clanging shut. "This is my office, not free twisty-bread night at Pizza Land."

*   *   *

Lucky for me, Dad came home late that night — so late that by the time he arrived, I'd already snuck off to bed, hoping that the next day he'd be in a better mood. Ben, on the other hand, waited up. He'd finally psyched himself up to face Dad with the truth, no matter what the consequences.

When Dad finally walked in the door, Ben was sitting in the living room. In the dark. As the door opened, Ben switched on the lamp just above his armchair — it was as if a single spotlight was illuminating him in the shadows.

"Hello, Dad," he said, in an unusually solemn voice. "We need to have a talk."

"I'm sorry," Dad said quickly. "I didn't mean to run over your bike. It was dark and —"

"You ran over my bike?" Ben asked, leaning forward.

"Um — no," Dad lied, pretending to be surprised Ben would even suggest such a thing. "That was stolen by local hoodlums."

Not to be distracted (even by so blatant a lie), Ben shook his head. "Dad, forget the bike. I have to tell you something."

Dad sat down in a chair across from Ben, who

suddenly lost his nerve. He tried to stall for time. It was so feeble — almost enough to make you feel a little sorry for him. But not quite. (Hey, did he feel sorry for me the day he broke the head off my doll and used it for his tabletop soccer game? I don't think so.)

"Mixed nuts?" Ben asked, offering Dad a bowl that's been on our coffee table since 1993.

"No, thanks," Dad said wisely, recoiling.

"Can I get you a warm glass of milk? Or maybe a nice herbal tea?"

"No, I'm fine," Dad assured him, obviously getting a little impatient.

"Are you *sure* you're comfortable?" Ben pressed. "Because you know I can get more pillows in the —"

"Ben! What is it?"

"I've been working at *Juice!*," Ben blurted, looking astonished that the words had come out of his mouth so easily. "That's why I didn't wanna work for you this year."

Dad furrowed his brow, silent.

"Ben, why didn't you just tell me?" he asked finally, sounding a little hurt.

"You always seem so excited about me working at your store," Ben explained. "Only, that's not where I see myself anymore." He looked down and began fidgeting with his fingers. It's what he always does when he's nervous. "I'm sorry. I just wanted to do my own thing."

Dad sighed, then shrugged his shoulders.

"Well, it's probably for the best, anyway," he acknowledged. "The place is a zoo. An entire cheer squad was there all day looking for pom-poms."

"Pom-poms?"

Oh, how I wish I had been there to see the look on Ben's face for myself when he heard that one. He was stuck in *Juice!* serving escapees from the retirement home, while Dad was juggling more cheerleaders than he could handle? Now, that's what I call getting what you deserve.

"We put in a whole section," Dad explained. "Next to the figure-skater tutus and tennis skirts. Female athletes are becoming the cornerstone of Singer Sporting Goods."

Ben looked like he was about to pass out. Dad stood up and put a hand on his shoulder. "Well. Good night, son."

He started to leave the room, and Ben waved weakly after him, too stunned to stand. "Tennis skirts?" he moaned. "Dad, wait . . . tennis skirts?"

Thomas Jefferson once said that "honesty is the first chapter in the book of wisdom." I think the second chapter must have been "It's Okay to Lie About Throwing the First Pie if It Will Keep Your Best Friend out of Plaid Jumpers."

Geena, Zach, and I had to pick up trash all day for Saturday detention. (Actually, I got two Saturdays for starting the pie toss.) But it wasn't so bad. We had these snazzy orange trash-collecting vests, professional trash-picking rods — and, of course, we had one another.

I even wrote a song for the occasion, and Geena and Zach *promised* me that they liked it. This time, I knew they weren't lying — because they sang along:

> *Tried to be honest as the day is long,*
> *Ended up in trouble, singing this song.*
> *Now my only friends are garbage and flies . . .*

I stopped singing and let Geena and Zach take the last line.

'Cause Addie went ballistic with Boston cream pies!

"Hey, Addie."

I looked up at the familiar voice, right into the face of Jake Behari. He was carrying a basketball. He must have been on his way to the courts behind the school. Just my luck. I blushed bright red. The last thing I wanted was for Jake to see me picking up trash along the side of the road. Could I look like a bigger loser?

But Jake didn't seem to care.

"Heard about the fight," he said, grinning. "Sorry I missed it — Boston cream pie's my favorite."

Was I imagining things, or did he actually sound *impressed*? I smiled back at him and opened my mouth to say something witty and clever and appealing about . . . trash collecting? Somehow, the situation didn't seem to lend itself to flirting. And as I racked my brains trying to come up with exactly the right response, he smiled, waved, and then walked away. Okay, so once again, I missed the chance to impress him with my sparkling personality — but on the other hand, he did come over to say hi to me. To *me*. That was definitely a step in the right direction.

"Did you guys see that?" I asked Geena and Zach, bubbling over with excitement. "Do you think he likes me?"

As they started to answer, I suddenly held up my hand to stop them.

"You know what? Never mind. Don't answer that." It may have taken a little pie — and a lot of cream — but I'd learned my lesson.

A few minutes after Jake left, we got more surprise visitors. But these two were much less welcome.

"Oh, is it Career Day?" Maris asked caustically, riding by on her shiny new pink bike. She wore a pink bike helmet to match. Cranberry, as always, was following close behind. She wore a blue helmet — but the mocking expression on her face was identical to Maris's.

I might have been embarrassed — if I hadn't noticed that Maris had a black eye. Courtesy of my Thomas Jefferson hat. You would think she would have learned her lesson, too. Apparently not.

"How nice of the school to give you a glimpse of your future," she continued, speeding by. "Later, you can come by and fish the leaves out of my swimming pool."

*   *   *

Too bad Maris was looking at me instead of at where she was going. If she'd been a little more careful, she might have noticed she was heading right toward a giant trash Dumpster. Her bike rammed right into it, and Maris flipped over the handlebars, landing in a heap in the middle of all the garbage.

"Aaaaaah!" she cried. When her head finally popped up over the edge, it was covered in garbage slop. She wiped a dollop of something slimy and green off her forehead and then, with a sigh, collapsed back into the mound of trash.

So, okay, she steered her bike safely around the Dumpster, and she and Cranberry rode off into the distance. You know what? Having them gone was a dream come true all by itself.

"Hey, Addie?" Zach called, rousing me from my little fantasy. He picked up a half-eaten sandwich from the ground and waved it in my face. I leaped away, just in time.

"Hungry?" he asked, smirking. "I'm sure there are at least a few bugs in here."

"Ew! Gross!" I swatted the trash picker away and ran off to hide behind Geena.

104

"Get away!" she cried, as he came after her next.

We both squealed with laughter and fear as Zach chased after us with the bug-infested sandwich. Saturday detention had never been so much fun.

I know it might not seem like the most picture-perfect start to seventh grade. I mean, we're only a few weeks into the school year and already I've taken a very public dip in a punch bowl, covered my social studies teacher in Boston cream pie, and gotten to know the contents of the Rocky Road Middle School garbage dump, up close and personal.

But like I say, I like to look on the bright side. And that's exactly what I'm going to do. It's been an *interesting* start to the year, at the very least, and I've got plenty of things to be thankful for:

1. Jake Behari knows my name.
2. Mr. Ward ended up giving us an "A" on our social studies assignment for doing such a good job "getting into character."
3. Now that Ben works at *Juice!,* maybe I can score a little-sister discount.
4. Did I mention Jake Behari knows my name?

Of course, the biggest thing to be thankful for is that, whatever seventh grade throws at me, I don't have to handle it alone. Geena and Zach will be by my side, the whole way through. And when the three of us are together, you can be sure of three things. Life will often be fun, sometimes even fabulous — and no matter what, it will *never* be boring.

Day after day is unfabulous
And everyone around me is unbearable
I'm gonna be the one unflappable
It's better unfabulous
It's better unfabulous
I'm gonna be the one unstoppable
It's better unfabulous

I'm gonna be the one unforgettable
It's better unfabulous
It's better unfabulous
I'm better unfabulous